OLIVER

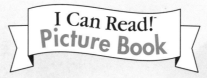

I Can Read!™
Picture Book

OLIVER

Story and pictures by Syd Hoff

Sandy Creek

Oliver
Copyright © 1960, 1988 by Syd Hoff

This 2010 edition licensed for publication by Sandy Creek
by arrangement with HarperCollins Publishers.

HarperCollins Publishers® and I Can Read Books® are registered trademarks.
All rights reserved. No part of this book may be used or reproduced in any manner whatsoever without
written permission except in the case of brief quotations embodied in critical articles and reviews. For
information concerning the text and illustrations, please contact HarperCollins Children's Books, a division
of HarperCollins Publishers, 10 East 53rd Street, New York, NY 10022.

Sandy Creek
387 Park Avenue South
New York, NY 10016

ISBN 978-0-7607-8396-2
Manufactured in China.
Manufactured 04/2012
Lot 12 13 SCP 10

OLIVER

Some elephants came across the ocean

on a ship.

They were going to work in the circus.

One elephant's name was Oliver.

7

When they landed

the circus man counted them:

8

"One, two, three, four, five,

six, seven, eight, nine, ten elephants."

9

"And one makes eleven," said Oliver.

"There must be a mistake.

I ordered only ten elephants,"

said the circus man.

"We don't need eleven."

11

"I won't take up much room,"

said Oliver.

"Elephants always do,"

said the circus man.

12

"Good-bye, Oliver,"

said the other elephants.

"Take good care of yourself."

13

Oliver was all alone.

He didn't know where to go.

A little mouse came along.

"Why don't you try the zoo?"

said the mouse.

"You look like the type they use there."

"Thanks, I'll go at once," said Oliver.

15

"Taxi!" said Oliver.

"What you need is a moving van,"

said the taxi man.

He did not stop.

16

Oliver followed the cars.

The drivers held out their hands

when they made a turn.

17

When Oliver made a turn

he held out his trunk.

18

He saw a woman weighing herself.

"My goodness,

I'm as heavy as an elephant," she said.

19

Oliver got on the scale.

"I'm heavy as an elephant, too,"

he said.

At last Oliver reached the zoo.

"Who is in charge here?" he asked.

"I am," said a man.

21

"Do you need an elephant?" asked Oliver.

"I'm sorry, not right now,"

said the zoo man.

"Thanks anyway," Oliver said

and walked away.

22

A man was selling peanuts.

"May I help you sell them?" asked Oliver.

"Would you sell them or eat them?"

asked the man.

"Eat them," said Oliver.

The man gave him some peanuts

for being honest.

23

Oliver left the zoo.

He walked down the street.

"Would anyone like to have me for a pet?"

he asked.

24

"I have a parakeet," said one person.

25

"I have goldfish," said another person.

26

"I have a cat," said another person.

"I have a duck," said someone else.

"I'd like a dog for a pet," said a lady.

29

"I can pretend I'm a dog," said Oliver.

"All right," she said.

Oliver and the lady went for a walk.

"Bowwow," said Oliver.

31

"What a nice dog," said the people.

"He's the biggest dog we ever saw!"

"I am hungry," said Oliver.

"Let's go home."

32

"Don't you have any hay?" he asked.

"No, but I have a nice bone,"

said the lady.

33

"Elephants need hay," Oliver said.

"I guess I can't be your dog after all.

But thank you, and good-bye."

"Good-bye," said the lady.

Oliver walked and walked.

Some people were riding horses.

Oliver watched.

35

"Horses get hay.

I wish I were a horse," he said.

36

"Do you need a horse?" asked Oliver.

"You look like an elephant.

But I'll ride you," said a man.

37

The man sat on Oliver's back.

"Giddyap," he said.

38

The horses jumped over the fence.

39

Plop!

Oliver could not jump over the fence.

"I guess I'm not a horse," he said.

"Good-bye."

"Good-bye," said the man.

40

Oliver passed a playground.

"May I play?" he asked.

"You may swing us," said the children.

41

"Is this the way?" asked Oliver.

"Not quite," said the children.

"But it will do."

42

"How does this work?" asked Oliver.

"It's a seesaw.

We'll get on the other side,"

said the children.

43

"Well?" asked Oliver.

The children rushed for the slide.

They couldn't all get on at once.

45

Oliver helped out.

It was time to rest.

The children talked about

what they wanted to be

when they grew up.

47

"I want to be a policeman," said Tommy.

"I want to be a nurse," said Mary.

49

"I want to be a cowboy," said Ben.

50

"I always wanted to work in the circus,"

said Oliver.

"I could be a dancing elephant."

51

He started to dance for the children.

Everybody stopped to watch.

They didn't see the circus parade coming.

They all watched Oliver.

53

They didn't see the acrobats.

They didn't see the jugglers.

They didn't see the clowns!

"Are they looking at me?"

asked the lion tamer.

"No," said the lion.

"They're looking at some elephant dancing."

"What's going on here?"

said the circus owner.

He ran over to look.

"That's the best dancing elephant
I've ever seen," he said.

59

"It's Oliver!" cried the other elephants.

60

"Oliver," said the circus man,

"I made a big mistake. We do need you.

Will you join the circus?"

61

"I'd love to," said Oliver.

"Hurray," cried the children.

"You got your wish!"

62

"Will you remember us?"

asked the children.

"Of course," said Oliver.

"An elephant never forgets."

63

"And even a rhinoceros

would remember the fun we had."

64